Kanvi

By

Laashya Naidu

Copyright Notice

© **Laashya Naidu & Dr. S.T. Naidu, 2025. All rights reserved.**

This book, including all its content, characters, and story, is **the intellectual property of the authors**. No part of this book may be **copied, reproduced, distributed, or transmitted** in any form—electronic, mechanical, photocopying, recording, or otherwise—without the **prior written permission** of both authors.

This work is **protected under copyright law**, and any unauthorized use, copying, or distribution **may lead to legal action**.

First Edition: 2025
For permissions, inquiries, or collaborations, contact:

Dr S T Naidu

drstnaid@gmail.com

Laashya Naidu

laashyanaidu@gmail.com

Author's words

Writing this book has been a journey filled with dreams, determination, and countless hours of imagination. It has tested my limits and stretched my creativity, yet it has also brought me immense joy and fulfilment. Each word, each chapter, holds a part of my soul, and every page tells a story that has been waiting to be told.

I am deeply grateful to my parents, whose love and support have been my greatest strength. Without them, this story would not exist. They have stood by me through every challenge, offering encouragement and wisdom that have shaped me into the person I am today. Their belief in me has been the foundation upon which this book stands.

To my readers—thank you for stepping into this world and giving life to these words. Your engagement and appreciation bring this story to life in ways I never imagined. You are the reason this journey continues, and for that, I am forever grateful.

This book is for all of you, and I hope it resonates in ways that inspire, challenge, and touch your heart.

With heartfelt gratitude,

Laashya

Contents

Chapter 1

The Weight of Words

"Kanvi! Wake up!"

A sharp knock rattled Kanvi's bedroom door, followed by her mother's exasperated voice. "The sun is already up, but you're still dreaming!"

Kanvi groaned and buried her face in the pillow. The dream was slipping away now, something about endless corridors, flickering torches, and whispers in an ancient tongue. It was always like this—books filled her days, and their stories crept into her nights.

"Kanvi!" Another knock, more insistent this time. "If you're late again, don't say I didn't warn you."

With a sigh, Kanvi pushed herself up, her thick hair falling messily over her shoulders. The morning light streamed through the window, illuminating the stacks of books scattered across her small room. Some were neatly piled on the wooden desk, others abandoned halfway through on the floor. A thick manuscript lay open beside her pillow, its yellowed pages lined with fading ink.

Her mother would call it an obsession. Kanvi called it a home.

"Coming," she mumbled, though she made no effort to hurry.

She ran a hand through her hair, her fingers catching in the tangled strands. Outside, the sound of bustling city filled the air, the hum of a city starting its day. But Kanvi wasn't interested in the world beyond her books. She had always been more at home in the past than in the present, losing herself in stories of forgotten empires and ancient prophecies.

She wished she could stay in bed, wrapped in the warmth of ink and parchment. But school—and her mother's patience—had limits.

Dragging herself up, she dressed quickly and stepped out of her room, bracing herself for another lecture.

(You see this is my life, I am the only daughter of my house and only kid too I don't have any siblings nor friends all of them were fake because either they love me for my looks or of my grades)

KANVI called her mother

(so she is my mother 'Kriti' she may look like an volcano but she is a flower garden , sounds funny right that's me guys, she has anger issues but that was never against me , I know she loves me but her love language is kind a tough row to hoe.)

Kanvi dad entered to her room he didn't shake her roughly nor call out loudly instead, he said "My darling come on sun has spread his feet, wake up love", kanvi stirred a bit. He gently brushed a stray strand of hair from Kanvi's forehead, his touch as light as a butterfly's wing. "Kanvi, my little star," he murmured, his voice a low, warm rumble. "It's time to wake up. The sun is eager to see your smile."

He paused, letting the melody and his words settle. Then, he lightly traced the curve of her cheek with his fingertip. "Come on, sleepyhead. The birds are singing just for you, and I've made your favourite pancakes."

A faint smile touched Kanvi's lips. She stirred, her eyelids fluttering. He leaned closer, his eyes sparkling with affection. "Open your eyes, Kanvi. Let's start a beautiful day together." Kanvi's eyelids fluttered open, her gaze soft and sleepy. A wide, genuine smile spread across her face as she recognized her father's familiar features. Without a word, she reached out and wrapped her arms around him, pulling him into a warm, lingering hug. He chuckled softly, returning the embrace with equal affection.

"Good morning, bubu," she mumbled, her voice still thick with sleep.

"Good morning, my sweet kuku," he replied, his hand gently stroking her hair.

Just as the warmth of the moment settled, a voice cut through the air, sharp and clear. "Look at the two of you! Still in bed? The sun is already high, and there's so much to do!"

Kanvi's mother stood in the doorway, hands on her hips, her expression a mix of exasperation and amusement. "Honestly," she continued, her voice rising slightly, "you two are impossible. Kanvi, you know you have your school today. And you," she turned to her husband, her tone softening slightly, "you're spoiling her. You'll never teach her discipline if you let her laze around like this, she is already a teen, when will she learn?"

"But, Maa," Kanvi began, her voice a soft protest, "dad was just..."

"Just what? Letting you waste precious time? I know, I know," her mother interrupted, shaking her head. "You two are always like this. It's like I'm the only one who cares about schedules and responsibilities."

She sighed, a hint of a smile playing on her lips. "Alright, alright. Enough with the cuddling. Kanvi, get ready. Your breakfast is on the table, and your school bus will be here soon. And you," she pointed a finger at her husband, "you're not getting off so easily, even if you have week off, There are errands to run, and the garden needs tending. Come on, both of you, move!"

(As I said my mom rules this house and let me arrange my books and get a shower or you know)

Kanvi tied her hair into a loose braid, staring at her reflection in the mirror. Her uniform—a crisp white skirt with a navy blue tee—felt stifling, like a costume she had to wear to fit into a world she didn't belong to.

Grabbing her school bag, she hurried to the dining table, where her mother was already waiting with breakfast. "You always wake up late, but somehow, you never forget to carry a book," her mother said, eyeing the thick novel tucked under Kanvi's arm.

Kanvi simply smiled and took a bite of her pancake. Books were her only escape.

By the time she reached school, the corridors were buzzing with students. That's when she spotted them—Sara and Daisy, her so-called friends. They were always sweet to her face, but Kanvi knew the truth. They only stuck around for one reason—her grades.

"Kanvi! Over here!" Daisy waved, flashing her usual fake smile.

Kanvi walked over, forcing a polite nod.

"You studied for the test, right?" Sara asked, linking her arm through Kanvi's. "You'll help us, won't you?"

Kanvi knew what they really meant—you'll let us copy, right?

She sighed inwardly but nodded. It was easier than dealing with their whispers behind her back. Because she had heard them before.

{"Kanvi acts so smart, but she's so boring."

"She thinks she's better than us just because she reads all the time."

"Let's be nice to her. We need her notes, after all."}

Kanvi knew the rumours they spread, but she never confronted them. What was the point? Real friendship wasn't something she had ever known.

As they walked to class, she adjusted the strap of her bag and looked at the sky. Somewhere, beyond these walls, beyond the expectations and fake smiles, there had to be something more.

She just didn't know that something was waiting for her—behind a forgotten door.

"Some people will only love you as long as they can use you. Their loyalty ends where the benefits stop."

Kanvi sat in the classroom, flipping through the pages of her history textbook, but her mind was elsewhere.

The air around her buzzed with chatter, but she had mastered the art of tuning it out—until Daisy's voice broke through.

"Oh my god, Kanvi, you won't believe what happened!" Daisy slid into the seat beside her, her eyes wide with fake concern. "Sara told everyone that you think you're too smart to be friends with us."

Kanvi blinked, gripping the edge of her book. "What?"

"I defended you, of course!" Daisy placed a hand on Kanvi's arm, squeezing it like she truly cared. "I told them you're just focused on studies, not arrogant. But, ugh, people love to twist things."

Kanvi knew better than to believe her. Daisy was an actress, a master of tears and sympathy. One moment she was the sweetest friend, the next, she was the victim—if things didn't go her way.

The bell rang, and Kanvi got up, but Daisy wasn't done.

"You're not upset, right?" she asked, her voice trembling, eyes shining as if she might cry. "You know I'd never betray you. You're my best friend, Kanvi."

"A snake sheds its skin, but it's still a snake."

Kanvi forced a smile. "Of course, Daisy."

But inside, something shifted. She had always let them use her, always ignored the whispers, but how long could she pretend not to hear the lies?

As Daisy linked arms with her, chattering away as if nothing had happened, Kanvi wondered—was this really friendship, or just another illusion?

And if it was an illusion, how much longer would she let herself be fooled?

"Some friendships are like chains—beautiful on the outside, but heavy on the soul."

Kanvi pressed her fingers against her temples, trying to focus on the teacher's voice. The class was silent except for the rhythmic scratching of pens on paper. But even in the quiet, she could hear them— Daisy and Sara, whispering behind her.

{"Did you hear? Kanvi got the highest again."

"She probably thinks she's better than us."

"She always acts so calm, but I bet she's full of herself."}

Kanvi gritted her teeth. They did this every time. When they needed her notes, they were the best of friends. But the moment they didn't, she became the villain in their story.

Still, she said nothing.

At lunch, Daisy found her again, flashing her usual bright smile. "Kanvi, sit with us! We missed you!"

Kanvi hesitated. Every part of her wanted to say no, to walk away and finally free herself from their web. But then Daisy pouted, eyes shimmering like she might cry. "You're not mad at us, right?"

"Guilt is the strongest weapon of manipulators."

Kanvi sighed and sat down. The moment she did, Daisy grinned like she had won a prize.

Throughout lunch, they laughed, gossiped, and acted like nothing had happened. Kanvi played along, but inside, she was exhausted.

She wasn't blind. She knew this wasn't real friendship. But maybe, just maybe, pretending was easier than being alone.

For now. This keeps Kanvi trapped in the cycle while building tension.

"The world may be harsh, but home is where love remains unchanged."

The moment Kanvi stepped into her house, a wave of relief washed over her. The fake smiles, the whispers, and the weight of being someone she wasn't—it all melted away.

Here, she didn't have to pretend.

"Kanvi, you're late!" her mother called from the kitchen, the sound of sizzling spices filling the air. "Come, freshen up before dinner."

Kanvi dropped her bag by the door and walked in, the warmth of home wrapping around her like a soft blanket. Her father sat on the couch, flipping through a newspaper, but the moment he saw her, his face lit up.

"How was school, kuku?" he asked, patting the seat beside him.

Kanvi sat down with a tired sigh. "The usual." Her mother peeked in from the kitchen. "Which means she's overthinking things again."

Kanvi smiled. They knew her too well. No matter how much she kept inside, her parents could always see through her and she can't and won't hide.

"You're doing too much for people who don't deserve it," her father said, tapping her head lightly. "Real friends don't make you feel lonely." Her mother nodded. "And you don't need to hold onto people just because they're there. Let them go."

Kanvi looked at them, feeling something tighten in her chest. If only it were that easy. But for now, she had this—her home, her parents, the only place in the world where she didn't have to prove herself. *"A person's behaviour is their real identity, not their words."*

Kanvi changed into her comfortable pyjamas and curled up in her bed, letting out a deep breath. The weight of the day still lingered, but here, in her quiet room, she could finally be herself.

She reached for the novel on her bedside table—an old book about Indian palaces, royal courts, and the people who lived within them. As she flipped through the pages, the words pulled her into another world. The story spoke of a grand empire, where kings ruled with wisdom, warriors fought with honour, and courtiers whispered secrets behind golden walls.

 But what caught Kanvi's attention the most was how people's behaviour shaped destinies.

A noble prince was betrayed not by his enemies, but by his closest friend. A wise queen lost everything because she trusted the wrong people. A brave soldier rose to greatness because he chose loyalty over deceit. "In history, and in life, people's actions speak louder than their promises."

Kanvi closed the book and stared at the ceiling.
Wasn't this the same in real life? Daisy and Sara
smiled at her, but their words were poison. They
acted like friends, but their actions proved
otherwise.

For so long, she had ignored it, thinking friendship
meant enduring flaws. But was it really friendship if
it left her feeling drained?

She ran her fingers over the book cover and sighed. If history had taught her anything, it was that trust was precious.

And maybe, just maybe, it was time to stop giving it away so easily, Tomorrow, she would still smile. She would still be kind. But she would no longer be blind.

Chapter 2

The Forgotten Door

"Dreams are whispers of the unseen, guiding us toward the unknown."

 Kanvi's routine remained the same—wake up, eat, read, and exist in a world where books were her only true escape. But ever since summer vacation started, something strange had begun happening.

At first, it was just in her dreams. A lotus, glowing faintly under the moonlight, swayed in the wind. Behind it stood a door—ancient, forgotten, waiting. Every night, it appeared, and every morning, she brushed it off as just another dream. But then, it started following her.

She would be walking in the park and suddenly spot a lotus carved into a stone bench. At a café, her fingers traced the design of a lotus unknowingly etched into the wooden table. Even in her own house, she found a faint outline of a door on her bedroom wall where there had been nothing before. "Coincidence," she told herself. But deep inside, doubt lingered.

To distract herself, she spent most of her time in the city library. It was her favourite place—a sanctuary where books held more meaning than real life. Here, she could travel through centuries, live in ancient palaces, and stand beside warriors without leaving her chair.

One afternoon, while exploring a rarely visited section, she ran her fingers over the spines of dusty, forgotten books. And then—her hand froze. A book with a deep blue cover, embroidered with a golden lotus. Her heart pounded. It looked just like the one in her dreams.

She hesitated, then slowly pulled it from the shelf. The moment she opened it, a chill ran down her spine. The first words on the page read:

"The door is waiting." Kanvi's breath hitched. This was no coincidence.

"Some mysteries find you when you least expect them."

Kanvi's fingers barely brushed against the book's cover when a shadow loomed over her. "That's not for you," a stern voice interrupted.

She turned sharply to see the librarian, an elderly woman with sharp eyes and an expression she couldn't quite read.

Before Kanvi could protest, the woman took the book from her hands, tucked it under her arm, and walked away without another word.

Kanvi stood frozen, her mind racing. "Not for me?" Since when did libraries restrict books like that?

She quickly followed, weaving between shelves, but the librarian was fast—too fast for someone her age. By the time Kanvi reached the front desk, the woman had disappeared.

Confused and frustrated, she turned to the assistant librarian. "Where's Mrs. Patel?" she asked, hoping for an answer.

The young woman frowned. "Who?" Kanvi blinked. "The librarian who just took a book from me. Elderly, strict-looking, always in a saree." The assistant chuckled. "Kanvi, I've worked here for three years. We don't have anyone like that." A chill crawled down Kanvi's spine.

She turned back toward the shelves, scanning the aisles. Empty. The book was gone. And so was the librarian.

"Not all who disappear are lost. Some are simply waiting to be found."

Kanvi's skin prickled as she stared at the assistant librarian, her mind refusing to accept what she had just heard.

"No," she muttered, shaking her head. "That's not possible. I saw her. She was right here."

The assistant gave her a concerned look. "Maybe you mistook a visitor for a librarian?"

Kanvi wanted to argue, but something inside her told her to stop. She had seen the woman. She had felt the weight of the book in her hands.

Then why did it feel like none of it had actually happened?

She turned back toward the shelves, her eyes searching for any trace of the old woman. The dusty aisles stretched endlessly, silent and undisturbed.

"The universe doesn't send warnings in words—it whispers in signs only the chosen can hear."

Before Kanvi could fully grasp what was happening, the heavy silence of the library was broken by a familiar voice. "Kanvi?"

She snapped her head up, her heart still racing. Her mother stood at the entrance, scanning the aisles with a concerned expression.

"It's getting late. Come on, let's go home." Kanvi hesitated, looking back at the book in her hands.

The words the old woman said —"You were never supposed to see this."—were still fresh.

But as her mother took a step closer, old woman reappeared Kanvi's breathe caught.

What was happening? She quickly shut her eyes, her fingers lingering for a moment before pulling away from the desk.

As they walked out of the library, the uneasiness didn't leave her. In fact, it grew stronger.

The sky had turned a strange shade of orange, even though it was past sunset.

The streetlights flickered, casting erratic shadows that didn't seem to match the movements around them. And then, it began.

First, a shop board creaked violently, even though the air was completely still.

Next, the sound of bells—soft, rhythmic, as if someone was walking behind them with anklets. But when Kanvi turned, no one was there.

And then—the most chilling thing of all.

A bus passed by, and in its window reflection, Kanvi saw something that made her freeze.

The old librarian. Standing just a few feet behind her. But when she turned around—nothing.

The old librarian. Standing just a few feet behind her. But when she turned around—nothing.

The old librarian. Standing just a few feet behind her. But when she turned around—nothing.

She wanted to tell her mother, but something held her back.

As they reached home, she knew one thing for sure. This wasn't just a dream anymore. The signs were real

The moment Kanvi stepped into her house, something felt off.

The air was colder than usual. Not the comforting coolness of an air-conditioned home—but an unsettling, bone-deep chill.

Her mother went into the kitchen, humming softly, oblivious to the strange shift in the atmosphere. But Kanvi? She felt it.

She set her bag down and glanced around. Everything looked the same—the familiar wooden shelves, the framed photographs, the soft glow of the living room lights. And yet, it felt different, like an invisible presence was lingering just beyond her sight.

Then—click.

The lights flickered.

Kanvi's breath hitched. She turned toward the hallway leading to her room. The door, which she always left slightly open, was now shut.

And for the first time ever, she hesitated before opening it.

Slowly, she reached out, her fingers grazing the cold metal of the doorknob. As she turned it, the door creaked open, revealing her dimly lit room. Everything was exactly as she had left it.

Except for one thing. The book.

The very same book from the library—the one she had returned—was sitting on her desk. Kanvi's heart pounded against her ribs. This was impossible. She had left it on the shelf.

She stepped closer, almost afraid to touch it. But before she could, something else caught her eye. Her mirror. She turned toward it, and her stomach dropped. There—on the reflection of her bed— someone was sitting.

 Kanvi spun around instantly, expecting to see a person. But her bed was empty. Her hands trembled as she turned back to the mirror. The figure was still there. Watching. And this time, it smiled.

Kanvi shook her head, trying to dismiss the strange visions that kept following her everywhere. It's just my imagination, she told herself. But deep down, she knew it wasn't.

That night, she lay on her bed, staring at the ceiling. The dreams had started again—the lotus, the door, the whisper of something ancient calling to her.

She turned to her bedside table, where she had placed a book about lost Indian palaces. The page she had bookmarked earlier now lay open, though she didn't remember flipping it.

And there, under a faded illustration of an ancient temple, she saw something she hadn't noticed before—

A door.

Not just any door.

The same one from her dreams.

Her breath caught as her fingers traced the outline of the drawing. This can't be a coincidence.

Just then, the wind outside howled, making her windows rattle. The lights flickered. And in that moment, Kanvi knew—

Whatever this was, it wasn't over. It was only just beginning.

Chapter 3

A Kingdom Lost to Time

"Some doors open to rooms. Others open to destinies."

Kanvi's heart pounded as she wandered through the vast library, her fingers trailing over the spines of books. The place was silent, except for the occasional creak of wooden shelves and the ticking of an old grandfather clock.

And then—she saw it.

A door.

The very same one from her dreams.

It stood at the farthest end of the library, hidden behind towering shelves. Unlike the others, it was carved with intricate lotus patterns and ancient symbols that seemed to shimmer under the dim light.

Her fingers trembled as she pushed it open.

A gust of warm air rushed past her, carrying the scent of sandalwood and roses. The room inside wasn't just a storage space—it was something else entircly.

At the centre stood a pedestal. And on it lay a book.

The cover was gold, embossed with unfamiliar inscriptions. As Kanvi stepped closer, a sudden rustling made her turn around.

She wasn't alone anymore.

They appeared like shadows at first, then took shape—men and women draped in silk, adorned with golden jewellery, their dark eyes piercing.

They looked like they had stepped out of an ancient Indian kingdom, their expressions unreadable

One of them, a woman with a crown-like headpiece, stepped forward. Her voice was smooth as flowing water.

"Only the worthy may claim the book. Prove yourself."

Kanvi swallowed hard. "How?"

The woman raised her hand, and suddenly, glowing inscriptions appeared in the air. Riddles.

The first one shimmered:

"I am not alive, yet I grow. I don't have lungs, yet I need air. What am I?"

Kanvi thought for a moment. Then it clicked. "Fire."

The letters dissolved. Another appeared.

"The more you take, the more you leave behind. What am I?"

She frowned, thinking hard. Then she whispered, "Footsteps."

The golden figures murmured among themselves, nodding in approval.

The final riddle flashed:

"I speak without a mouth and hear without ears. I have no body, but I come alive with wind. What am I?"

Kanvi hesitated. The answer danced on the tip of her tongue. Then she gasped. "An echo."

A hush fell over the room. The woman smiled.

"You have proven yourself."

Kanvi barely had time to scream.

The moment she opened the book, a golden light burst from its pages, wrapping around her like a whirlwind. The library vanished, swallowed by an endless swirl of ink and ancient symbols.

She felt herself falling—faster, deeper—until suddenly…

She landed with a thud.

The scent of wet earth and jasmine filled her nostrils. The air was warm, carrying the distant sound of temple bells and bustling streets. As she lifted her head, her eyes widened in disbelief.

She wasn't in the library anymore.

Before her stretched a grand city of towering stone palaces, gleaming temples, and streets lined with merchants selling silk and spices.

The sky was painted gold by the setting sun, and people dressed in traditional attire moved with a grace she had only seen in history books.

A magnificent fort loomed in the distance, its golden domes shining under the sunlight.

And then, she saw the royal emblem.

Her heart skipped a beat.

Vijayanagar.

She had read about it—the glorious empire ruled by the legendary Krishna Devaraya, one of the greatest kings of India. But this wasn't just history. This was real. Kanvi stumbled forward, trying to process what had happened. That's when she heard voices.

"Who is she?

"She's dressed strangely."

"She must be a spy!"

Kanvi turned to see a group of soldiers approaching her, their hands resting on the hilts of their swords. Their leader, a tall man with sharp eyes, stepped forward.

"You! State your name and purpose."

Kanvi opened her mouth, but no words came out. What was she supposed to say? That she fell into a book and ended up in the past?

The soldiers exchanged glances, growing impatient.

"Take her to the palace," the leader commanded.

Before Kanvi could protest, they seized her arms and started marching toward the grand fort. Panic surged through her.

She had dreamed of seeing history.

She never thought she'd be trapped inside it.

Kanvi's heart pounded as she twisted free from the soldiers' grip and ran. The long stone corridors of the palace stretched endlessly before her, their golden carvings glowing under the oil lamps. The scent of sandalwood filled the air, but she had no time to take in the grandeur.

She needed to escape.

Her bare feet skidded across the polished floor as she turned a sharp corner— and crashed straight into someone.

The impact sent her stumbling back, but before she could fall, a strong yet gentle hand caught her arm.

"Ah, child, slow down. The palace is not a place for such haste," a deep, amused voice said.

Kanvi looked up and froze.

Before her stood a man dressed in simple yet elegant robes, his forehead marked with sacred lines of vibhuti. His dark eyes held a mischievous twinkle, as if he knew secrets no one else did. A soft smile played on his lips.

It took Kanvi only a second to recognize him.

Pandit Ramakrishna.

The brilliant, wise, and playful poet-scholar of Krishna Devaraya's court.

A wave of emotions hit her—excitement, disbelief, admiration. Before she could stop herself, she flung her arms around him.

"Pandit Ramakrishna!" she exclaimed.

The scholar stiffened in surprise, but Kanvi didn't care. She was hugging history itself.

Then, realizing what she had just done, she quickly pulled back, her face turning red.

Ramakrishna chuckled, his sharp eyes studying her. "You speak as if we are old friends, yet I do not recall meeting you before, young lady. Who are you?"

Kanvi gulped. How could she explain? But she had no choice.

"Pandit-ji," she whispered, stepping closer. "I am not from here. I am from… another time."

For the first time, Ramakrishna's playful gaze turned serious. "Another time?"

She nodded frantically. "I was in my library—then I found this book—and then I was here! I don't know how or why, but I need help. Please!"

Ramakrishna was silent for a moment, then smiled. "Fascinating. And what proof do you have of this claim, my mysterious visitor from time itself?"

Kanvi hesitated. Then, she reached into her pocket and pulled out a small, rectangular object. Her phone.

Ramakrishna took it, turning it curiously in his hands. "A box of mirrors?"

Kanvi sighed. "It's called a phone. It's from the future."

Ramakrishna tilted his head, intrigued. Then, he returned it to her and grinned. "Well, this is a problem unlike any I have faced before. But I do love a challenge."

Kanvi's eyes lit up. "You believe me?"

He laughed. "I believe in things beyond understanding. Come, let us solve this mystery together."

For the first time since she arrived, Kanvi felt hope.

Kanvi walked beside Pandit Ramakrishna, her heart pounding in her chest. The palace hallways were grand, with intricately carved pillars and golden torches flickering against the walls. Servants and guards bowed as they passed, whispering among themselves.

And then, as they stepped into the royal court, Kanvi's breath caught in her throat.

There, seated upon the grand simhasana (throne), was Sri Krishna Devaraya.

The king radiated power and grace, his broad shoulders draped in a silk shawl, his sharp eyes scanning the room with quiet authority. His skin glowed under the golden lights, his long hair tied neatly, and his presence alone commanded respect. He was no ordinary ruler—he was a warrior, a scholar, a legend.

Kanvi had read about him in history books, but seeing him in person was something else entirely.

Before Ramakrishna could introduce her, words flowed from Kanvi's lips like poetry.

"Oh mighty king, whose strength rivals the gods,

In wisdom and valour, you stand against all odds.

Your throne, a beacon of justice and grace,

Your name, a legacy time cannot erase."

The court fell silent. Every eye turned to her.

Krishna Devaraya leaned forward, intrigued. "Who is this girl with a tongue as sharp as a poet's quill?"

Kanvi quickly glanced at Ramakrishna for help.

To her shock, the great scholar grinned mischievously and bowed.

"Maharaj, allow me to introduce Kanvi, a dear friend of Sharda Devi—my wife. She is a poetess of remarkable talent."

Kanvi's eyes widened in horror. What?! His wife's friend?!

The king's expression softened with amusement. "A friend of Sharda Devi? Then you are most welcome in Vijayanagar, dear Kanvi."

Kanvi opened her mouth to protest, but Ramakrishna subtly pinched her wrist, signalling her to stay silent.

The king rose from his throne and walked toward her. "A poetess should be tested before she is honoured. Kanvi, tell me, what does beauty mean to you?"

Kanvi swallowed, then lifted her chin and replied,

"Beauty is not just in gold or silk so fine,

It shines in truth, in a heart divine.

A face may fade, but deeds remain,

A soul untouched by greed or gain."

A slow smile spread across Krishna Devaraya's face.

"Well spoken," he said. "You have impressed me, Kanvi."

Kanvi let out a breath she didn't realize she was holding.

Ramakrishna, still smirking, whispered, "You are now under royal favour, my dear poetess. That is the safest place to be in a strange land."

Kanvi took a deep breath, her heart racing as she looked at the magnificent Krishna Devaraya. He was unlike any king she had ever imagined—strong, powerful, yet carrying an air of wisdom and kindness. His sharp features, commanding posture, and deep, intelligent eyes made him the perfect ruler, a man of both strength and heart, there was something about him that demanded honesty. His presence, his aura—it was overwhelming.

Ramakrishna, standing beside her, chuckled softly and whispered, "Careful, Kanvi. Krishna Devaraya let out a rich, amused laugh. "It is rare to find a poetess so fearless.

A murmur of admiration swept through the court. Even the ministers, who rarely showed emotion, nodded in approval.

Krishna Devaraya's smile deepened. "Kanvi, you see not only with your eyes but with your soul. I welcome you to Vijayanagar."

Kanvi exhaled, feeling the weight of his words. She had just spoken her heart, but now she realized—

She had stepped into history.

And history… was watching her closely.

Kanvi followed Pandit Ramakrishna through the bustling streets of Vijayanagar. The air was filled with the scent of fresh flowers, incense, and the distant chatter of merchants selling silk and spices. She couldn't believe she was walking through history—real, living history.

After what felt like an endless walk, they arrived at a simple yet beautiful house. Compared to the grand palace, it was cosy, surrounded by trees, with a small tulsi plant in the courtyard.

Before Ramakrishna could knock, the door burst open—

And there stood Sharada Devi, hands on her hips, eyes narrowed.

"You! Rama! Do you even remember you have a home? Or should I start renting it out to travellers?"

Kanvi bit her lip to hold back a laugh.

Ramakrishna grinned, completely unaffected. "Oh, my Sharada! What a blessing to hear your sweet voice scolding me first thing after returning home!"

Sharada scoffed. "Who is this?" she asked, eyeing Kanvi.

Kanvi stepped forward and smiled politely. "I am Kanvi, your husband's—"

Before she could explain, Ramakrishna interrupted, smirking. "She's your long-lost sister!"

Kanvi gasped, while Sharada's eyes widened in shock.

"My—what?! Ramakrishna, you—" She turned to Kanvi and dramatically grabbed her hands. "Where were you all these years, my dear sister? Did this horrible husband of mine keep you hidden?"

Kanvi burst out laughing. "No, no, I'm just—"

But before she could finish, another voice called out.

"Rama! Is that you?"

An elderly woman, draped in a simple saree, stepped out of the house—Ramakrishna's mother, Laxmi Maa. She looked at Kanvi with kind but mischievous eyes.

"Who is this girl? Another one of your pranks, Rama?"

Kanvi was about to protest, but Sharada gasped dramatically again.

"Amma! Rama finally did something good in his life! He found my long-lost sister!"

Laxmi Maa's eyes twinkled with amusement. She clasped Kanvi's face. "Oh, poor child! You look just as troubled as me, living in this mad house.

Kanvi couldn't control her laughter anymore. The whole scene was absolutely ridiculous. She had landed in the most chaotic, hilarious household in all of Vijayanagar! And honestly? She loved it.

As night fell, the warm glow of oil lamps illuminated Tenali Rama's house. The aroma of freshly prepared food filled the air as Sharada bustled around, setting the plates with her usual lively charm.

Kanvi, still overwhelmed by the day's events, sat beside her, watching in amusement as Sharada playfully scolded Rama for something trivial.

"Rama! You think you are the greatest poet and scholar in Vijayanagara, but you cannot even remember to bring the tamarind I asked for?" Sharada huffed, folding her arms.

Rama, ever the witty one, chuckled. "Oh, my dear Sharada, why worry about tamarind when you already bring enough spice to my life?" He winked at Kanvi, who stifled a laugh.

Just then, Laxmi Maa, entered with her walking stick, as they sat down for dinner, Kanvi couldn't help but admire the warmth of the household. The playful banter between Rama and Sharada, loving nature of Laxmi Maa—it all felt so familiar, so real.

Between bites of delicious food, Kanvi whispered to Rama, "I still don't understand how I got here… or why I keep seeing that lotus and mysterious door. There must be a reason."

Rama, his eyes twinkling with intrigue, replied, "Then we shall solve this mystery together. But first—more food!"

Sharada laughed, serving another helping, and for the first time since arriving in this strange, historical world, Kanvi felt a little less lost.

But little did she know, the real adventure was only just beginning

Chapter 4

The Prophecy's Shadow

The night was thick with silence, yet Kanvi's heart pounded like a battle drum. The air in Ramakrishna's house was warm and comforting, but her thoughts were tangled in whispers of the unknown. The lotus, the forgotten door, the golden book—all of it led to something she couldn't yet understand.

She lay awake, staring at the wooden beams above her. The candle on the bedside table flickered slightly, its flame dancing in the stillness. Sleep refused to claim her. She felt as though something—or someone—was watching.

Then it happened.

A sudden gust of wind blew through the open window, snuffing out the candle. The room was plunged into darkness, and for a brief moment, Kanvi swore she saw a shadow move in the corner.

Her breath hitched.

She sat up, gripping the edges of the blanket. "Who's there?" she whispered, but only silence answered.

She hesitated before swinging her legs over the cot and stepping onto the cool stone floor. The faint glow of moonlight seeped through the window, casting eerie shapes across the room. Slowly, cautiously, she moved toward the door.

And then, she heard it.

A voice—low and ancient—whispering her name.

Kanvi.

Her pulse roared in her ears. She turned sharply, her eyes scanning the darkness, but she saw nothing. Only the sound of her own shallow breathing filled the space. Yet the voice had been real. It had called her.

Mustering her courage, she stepped outside into the courtyard. The air was thick with the scent of jasmine, and the palace lights in the distance twinkled like fallen stars.

But then—

A figure stood beneath the neem tree.

Kanvi's breath caught. Draped in robes darker than the night, the figure exuded an otherworldly presence. Their face was obscured, yet their eyes—piercing and golden—shone through the darkness.

"You have touched the book of destiny," the figure said, voice echoing like a forgotten prophecy. "The path has been set. There is no turning back."

Kanvi clenched her fists. "Who are you?"

The figure tilted their head slightly, as if amused. "That is not the question you should be asking."

A chill ran down Kanvi's spine. "Then what should I ask?"

The figure took a step forward, and suddenly, the wind picked up, rustling the leaves above them.

"You should ask why the book chose you."

Kanvi swallowed hard. She had been wondering the same thing. Of all the people in the world, why was she the one who had stumbled into this mystery?

Before she could speak, the figure raised a hand. "The kingdom of Vijayanagar is on the brink of a fate unknown. Shadows lurk in places unseen, and deception wears the face of loyalty. The prophecy speaks of a girl who walks between time, whose heart carries both wisdom and fire."

Kanvi's mind whirled. "A prophecy?"

"The prophecy's shadow," the figure murmured. "And you, Kanvi… you are standing at its very heart."

Kanvi took a step back. "I don't understand. What prophecy?"

But the figure was already fading, their form dissolving into the night like mist. Only their final words remained, carried on the wind—

"The past and future are but mirrors. What is broken once can be broken again."

And then, they were gone.

Kanvi stood frozen, her mind racing. The golden book, the lotus, the forgotten door—everything was leading her toward something much bigger than herself. Something she wasn't sure she was ready for.

But fate had already chosen her.

And now, she had no choice but to follow the path it laid before her.

"Wisdom, when wrapped in laughter, stays in the heart forever."

From the day Kanvi stepped into Pandit Ramakrishna's home, life had been a whirlwind of lessons, laughter, and unexpected wisdom.

Each morning, before the city of Vijayanagar fully awakened, she would follow Rama to the royal court of Sri Krishna Devaraya.

At first, she assumed she would merely observe the grand proceedings—watch history unfold as a silent spectator. But Vijayanagar was not a place for mere spectators.

Every day, a new case was presented before the king, and with each case came a lesson—one wrapped not in long sermons, but in sharp wit and humour, courtesy of the kingdom's most brilliant mind: Tenali Rama.

But if court was where wisdom was learned, home was where comedy reigned.

If the royal court was where Rama displayed his intelligence, home was where he met his greatest challenge—his wife, Sharada Devi.

The moment they stepped inside, she was waiting, arms folded, eyes narrowed. The scent of fresh tamarind curry filled the house, but the tension in the air made it clear—Rama had once again done something to earn a scolding.

Sharada had a remarkable ability to turn even the simplest of questions into a verbal duel.

"What foolishness did you commit today, Pandit-ji?" she demanded, before even allowing him to sit down.

Kanvi, now familiar with the daily routine, took a seat at the corner of the room, silently enjoying the entertainment.

Rama, ever the performer, sighed dramatically, placing a hand over his heart. He spoke of how he had saved the mango thief from the cruel fate of punishment, how he had ensured justice while also enriching the village with more trees. Surely, such noble acts deserved a warm welcome home?

Sharada was unmoved.

Instead, she pointed to the growing collection of strange objects in the corner of their house— evidence from past court cases. A broken clay pot, a single wooden spoon, a pile of coins that no longer held value. Each one, she reminded him, had been acquired due to one of Rama's brilliant "solutions" in court.

Kanvi, suppressing her laughter, observed how, despite all her complaints, there was something affectionate in the way Sharada argued.

This wasn't true anger—it was a dance. A routine as old as their marriage.

And though Rama protested dramatically, though he clutched his heart and proclaimed himself a victim of constant criticism, there was a twinkle in his eye as he did so.

He would take every argument, every scolding, if it meant hearing his wife's voice fill their home.

Kanvi had once believed wisdom was found in books, buried in ancient texts and scholarly discussions. But ever since she began accompanying Tenali Rama to court, she realized something—wisdom was everywhere. It was hidden in ridiculous disputes, absurd complaints, and, most commonly, in the sarcastic banter between Rama and Sharada Devi.

Each day in court brought a new case, and each case came with a lesson—though wrapped in such humour that Kanvi often wondered if Rama was solving problems or just entertaining himself.

But beneath the laughter, the wisdom remained.

Lesson 1: People Will Always Find a Way to Blame Others

One morning, the royal court was filled with murmurs as a nobleman stormed in, holding a broken pot over his head. His silk robes fluttered dramatically as he declared his misery to the king.

"Maharaj, my expensive pot of ghee was shattered! My servant is to blame!"

A frail old man stood beside him, trembling like a leaf in the wind.

"Forgive me, Maharaj!" the servant pleaded. "But I did not break it! The pot slipped from the nobleman's own hands!"

The nobleman scoffed. "Lies! If he had cleaned the floor properly, I would not have tripped! And if the pot maker had made a sturdier pot, it would not have broken!"

Kanvi blinked. *"Wait… so now even the pot maker is guilty?"*

The nobleman continued, "And if the weather had not been so humid, my hands would not have been sweaty, and the pot would not have slipped!"

The court erupted into murmurs.

Rama, who had been quietly grinning, finally stood up. "Ah, Maharaj, this is indeed a serious matter. We must punish the true culprit—"

The court held its breath.

"THE SUN!" Rama declared.

The nobleman frowned. *"The… sun?"*

"Of course!" Rama exclaimed. "The sun caused the heat. The heat made your hands sweaty. Your sweaty hands dropped the pot. It is clear—the sun must be punished!"

Even the king let out an amused chuckle. The nobleman turned red, realizing how foolish his accusations sounded.

Kanvi whispered to Rama, "So the lesson is…?"

Rama smiled. "People will blame anything and everything before taking responsibility for their own mistakes."

And just like that, the case was dismissed.

Lesson 2: Greed Always Digs Its Own Grave

On another occasion, a wealthy merchant approached the court, furious.

"Maharaj! My neighbour buried a chest of gold in his garden, and when I dug up my own garden, I found nothing!"

The king raised an eyebrow. "And why did you expect to find gold in your garden?"

"Because if my neighbour has gold, surely I should have some too!"

Kanvi nearly choked on the water she was drinking.

Rama sighed dramatically. "Ah, greed is such a tragic disease. This poor man is suffering greatly!"

The merchant beamed, thinking Rama was supporting him. "Yes! Yes! My suffering is endless!"

"Then we must treat it immediately," Rama continued. "Guards! Please bring a shovel. Let us dig up his entire house. Perhaps his greed will turn into gold!"

The merchant turned pale. "No, no, that won't be necessary!"

"Are you sure?" Rama asked innocently. "Perhaps we should dig up your neighbour's house too. Maybe you think his wife and children belong to you as well?"

The merchant, now sweating, stammered, "That's ridiculous!"

"Exactly!" Rama said with a grin. "Greed is ridiculous. Be happy with what you have, or prepare to lose even that."

The merchant, realizing his foolishness, bowed and left.

Kanvi smirked. Another lesson, another victory.

Lesson 3: The Smartest Person in the Room is usually the Quietest

One evening, Rama and Kanvi returned home, exhausted from the endless absurdities of the court. But peace was an illusion in the house of Pandit Ramakrishna.

Sharada Devi was waiting, her arms crossed, and her foot tapping impatiently.

"Rama, where have you been?"

Rama straightened his back. "Solving the kingdom's problems, my dear!"

Sharada narrowed her eyes. "And what about the problem of you forgetting to bring the rice I asked for this morning?"

Kanvi bit her lip, hiding her smile.

Rama cleared his throat. "Ah… you see, my dearest, I was so busy contemplating matters of justice and fairness that I forgot this small household duty."

Sharada scoffed. "Fairness? Should I be fair and forget to cook dinner too?"

Rama's confidence faltered. "Now, now, my lotus of the house, let's not take such drastic measures—"

"In fact," Sharada continued, "why don't you solve the problem of hunger **yourself** since you are so wise?"

At this point, Kanvi was struggling to hold back her laughter.

Laxmi Maa, who had been quietly knitting in the corner, finally looked up.

"Rama, my son… you talk too much."

Silence.

Rama, for the first time in years, had nothing to say.

Kanvi turned to Sharada. "That… was the most powerful statement I've heard all day."

"That's because the smartest people in the room,"

Sharada said, smirking, "are usually the ones who don't waste words."

Kanvi mentally noted another lesson—sometimes, silence was the most effective response.

Rama sighed and picked up a basket. "I shall go buy rice, my dear."

Sharada nodded, satisfied.

"And while you're at it," she added, "get me some tamarind too."

Rama paused at the door, muttering to Kanvi, "One day, I will win an argument in this house."

"Not today," Kanvi replied, laughing.

Days turned into weeks, and Kanvi realized something: wisdom wasn't just found in long discourses or books. It was hidden in everyday moments.

It was in the way Rama twisted foolishness into lessons. In the way Sharada subtly kept her husband's ego in check. In the way Laxmi Maa never raised her voice, yet always had the final word.

She had travelled through time, expecting to find grand history. Instead, she found something greater—practical wisdom, wrapped in humour and love.

That night, as she lay in bed, she smiled.

She had not just learned about justice and fairness.

She had learned about life.

And if laughter was part of that lesson, she welcomed it with open arms.

"The moment you stop seeking validation, you become truly free."

Kanvi had come to Vijayanagar expecting history, expecting wisdom wrapped in tradition. She had not expected *this*—a daily rollercoaster of humour, wit, and strangely insightful life lessons from the kingdom's greatest troublemaker, Tenali Ramakrishna.

She spent every day in the royal court, watching cases unfold. Some were serious, but most were ridiculous—villagers fighting over a stray cow, a nobleman accusing a sparrow of stealing his pearls, a shopkeeper claiming his shadow was being sold along with his wares.

At first, Kanvi had been fascinated. Then she had been amused. And now? Now, she had realized something far more important.

Most people were **foolish**. And the only way to live peacefully was to **ignore them as much as possible.**

Chapter 5

The Midnight Enigma

"Some mysteries must be solved, but some... are better left undisturbed."

Kanvi had seen many strange things in her time at Vijayanagar—noblemen arguing over stolen mangoes, merchants demanding laws for their own egos, and, of course, the daily battlefield that was Rama and Sharada's marriage.

But nothing had prepared her for what happened on that one fateful midnight.

It all started with a whisper.

A Shadow in the Dark

The night was still. The streets of Vijayanagar were bathed in moonlight, the oil lamps flickering in the soft breeze. Kanvi sat by the window in Rama's house, lost in thought, when she saw it.

A shadow.

It darted past the narrow alley, moving fast—too fast for a human.

Kanvi's breath hitched. Was it just a trick of the light? She leaned forward, her eyes scanning the street. And then—she saw it again.

This time, the shadow stopped.

For a fleeting moment, she could make out a cloaked figure standing at the edge of the marketplace.

And then, in the blink of an eye, it disappeared.

Kanvi's heart pounded. Who—or what—was that?

Without thinking, she rushed to wake Rama.

The Master Detective (Or So He Thought)

Kanvi shook Rama awake. "Rama! Get up! There's something outside!"

Rama groaned, rolling over. "Ah, my dear poetess, the only thing outside at this hour is sleep, and I was enjoying it deeply!"

Kanvi grabbed a pillow and smacked him on the head. "No time for jokes! I saw something!"

Now, that got his attention. Rama sat up, rubbing his forehead. "You saw something? What kind of something? A thief? A ghost? Sharada looking for missing tamarind?"

"A shadow," Kanvi whispered. "Moving unnaturally fast." That woke him up completely.

"A shadow, you say?" he mused, stroking his chin. "Well, Kanvi, we have only one choice—"

Sharada's voice cut through the darkness.

"Yes, yes, we go investigate. I'm coming too."

Kanvi turned, startled. "Sharada?! What are you doing awake?"

Sharada folded her arms. "Please. Do you think I'd let you two run around the city alone at midnight? If there's danger, I need to be there—to make sure Rama doesn't do something stupid."

Rama gasped. "My love! What an insult! Have I ever done anything reckless?"

Sharada raised an eyebrow. "Last week, you tried to climb a tree to catch a talking parrot because you thought it was a messenger from the gods."

Kanvi blinked. "Wait… that actually happened?"

Sharada sighed. "Yes. Unfortunately."

Ignoring the embarrassment, Rama straightened his robes. "Well then! Let us embark on a grand adventure into the night!"

And so, the trio sneaked out of the house, unaware that they were walking straight into a trap.

The streets of Vijayanagar were eerily silent as they followed the shadow's last known path. Kanvi led the way, her eyes scanning every corner. Rama, however, was more focused on narrating their journey dramatically.

"Three brave souls set forth into the unknown, facing dangers unseen, guided only by the moonlight!"

Sharada smacked him on the arm. "Less talking, more looking!"

They followed the trail until they reached an old, forgotten shrine at the outskirts of the city. The place had been abandoned for years, overgrown with vines, its stone walls cracked with age.

But something was off.

A soft glow flickered inside.

Kanvi exchanged nervous glances with Rama and Sharada. "Someone's inside."

Rama took a deep breath. "Only one way to find out."

They stepped forward—

And the doors slammed shut behind them.

The room was plunged into darkness. A cold breeze swept through, making the oil lamps flicker.

Kanvi's pulse quickened. "That… was not the wind."

Rama nodded. "I have a feeling we are not alone."

And then—

A whisper.

Not a human whisper, but something deeper, something ancient.

"Why have you come here?"

The voice echoed from nowhere and everywhere. The shadows on the walls twisted unnaturally.

Sharada, despite everything, crossed her arms. "I knew following you two was a bad idea."

Rama, ever the brave fool, took a step forward. "We are but humble travellers! If we have disturbed you, we deeply apologize!"

A low chuckle filled the room. "Apologies will not save you now."

Kanvi's breath caught in her throat. Was this… a spirit? A curse? A trick?

Suddenly, the glow brightened, revealing something terrifying—

A figure in a dark robe, face hidden beneath a hood.

"You seek answers," the figure murmured. "But some truths should remain buried."

Kanvi's heart pounded. "Who are you?"

The figure stepped closer. "I am the keeper of forgotten things. And you—"The hooded face turned towards Rama and said "you are a fool."

Sharada smirked. "Finally, someone agrees with me."

But the joke did little to ease the fear in the air.

The figure raised a hand, and suddenly—the floor beneath them began to crack.

"Leave now, or be swallowed by the past!"

Without hesitation, Rama grabbed Kanvi's arm. "Right! Time to go!"

They ran.

As they reached the door, Sharada turned back. "Wait! Who are you really?"

For the first time, the figure's hood slipped slightly—just enough for them to glimpse a pair of piercing silver eyes.

"You will know soon enough," the figure whispered. "When the prophecy comes true."

And then—everything went black.

Kanvi woke up to the sound of birds. Sunlight streamed through the windows. She was… back in Rama's house.

Had it all been a dream?

But then she saw them—Rama and Sharada, both sitting at the table, eyes wide, faces pale.

"So," Rama said weakly. "That happened."

Sharada nodded. "That definitely happened."

Kanvi sat up. "Who was that? What prophecy were they talking about?"

No one had an answer.

But as they sat in silence, one thing was clear.

The mystery was only beginning.

And next time, they might not escape so easily. Morning in Vijayanagar usually meant the lively sounds of merchants, the aroma of fresh jasmine, and the distant hum of temple bells. But in Tenali Rama's house, it meant three people sitting in absolute silence, trying to process what had happened the night before.

Kanvi stared at the burn mark on her wrist—proof that what she had seen wasn't a dream. Rama drummed his fingers on the table, deep in thought. Sharada, for once, wasn't scolding anyone.

Something had changed.

Someone had spoken of a prophecy.

And worst of all, they had seen his eyes.

The Silver-Eyed Stranger

The figure from the shrine haunted Kanvi's thoughts. Those piercing silver eyes, that cryptic warning, the shadows that seemed alive. Who was he? And what had he meant by "when the prophecy comes true"?

"Rama," Kanvi finally broke the silence, "what do we do now?"

Rama sighed dramatically. "My dear poetess, I was hoping the problem would just… disappear if I ignored it."

Sharada rolled her eyes. "Of course. Just like how you ignored our neighbour's goat eating my saree last week?"

"Ah, but my love," Rama said with a grin, "wasn't it a great way to test if your saree was made of pure silk?"

"Rama!" Sharada picked up a ladle and swung at him. He barely dodged.

"Fine, fine!" Rama held up his hands in surrender. "We investigate. But we must be careful."

Kanvi frowned. "Why?"

Rama leaned in, his usual playfulness gone. "Because if someone like him—someone with silver eyes—wants to keep a secret buried, then digging too deep might get us buried with it."

The words sent a chill through the air.

Chapter 6

The Forbidden Name

Determined to find answers, the trio headed to the Vijayanagar royal archives—a place filled with ancient texts, scrolls, and knowledge that most people had long forgotten.

The royal librarian, an elderly man with eyebrows so thick they looked like sleeping caterpillars, greeted them with suspicion.

"Pandit-ji, why are you here? You only visit when you need trouble."

"Me? Trouble?" Rama gasped dramatically. "You wound me, good sir! I merely wish to study history!"

The librarian snorted but allowed them inside.

As they searched through dusty scrolls, Kanvi found something unusual—a book titled "The Lost Shadows of Vijayanagar."

It was old. Very old. The pages crumbled at her touch. But as she flipped through, she froze.

There. On one of the pages.

A rough sketch of a hooded figure with silver eyes.

The caption read:

"The last known guardian of the Forgotten Prophecy, lost to time. The one who walks in shadows."

Kanvi's breath caught. "It's him."

But before she could read further, the librarian suddenly snatched the book from her hands.

"Enough," he said sternly. "You must not go any further."

Rama stepped forward, his usual humour gone. "Why not?"

The librarian hesitated, then whispered:

"Because those who seek the Whispering Prophecy never return."

Back at home, the weight of the discovery settled on them.

"A prophecy so dangerous that it was erased from history?" Kanvi murmured.

"And a silver-eyed man guarding it," Sharada added.

"Which means," Rama concluded, "we have two choices. One: pretend we never saw anything and live our lives happily—"

Kanvi and Sharada glared at him.

"—or two," he sighed, "we find out what this prophecy is before it finds us."

The decision was made. They needed answers.

That night, they sought out the only person in Vijayanagar who might know the truth.

A mysterious old woman named Devi Amara.

She lived on the outskirts of the city, near the abandoned ruins of an ancient temple. People whispered that she knew things no one else dared to speak of.

They arrived at her small hut, only to find her already waiting for them.

"So," she said, her voice low, "you have seen the Silver-Eyed Guardian."

Kanvi's heart pounded. "You know him?"

Devi Amara nodded.

"He is not a man. He is a warning."

She leaned forward, her voice barely above a whisper.

"And the prophecy he guards… is about to come true." The night was thick with tension as Devi Amara's words echoed in their ears.

"The prophecy he guards… is about to come true."

Kanvi shivered. Rama, for once, was speechless. Even Sharada, who usually had a sharp remark ready, looked unsettled.

"What prophecy?" Kanvi finally asked.

Devi Amara sighed and reached for an old wooden box. From inside, she pulled out a tattered scroll, its edges burnt, its ink faded.

"This," she whispered, "is the last known record of the Whispering Prophecy."

With trembling fingers, Kanvi unrolled it.

The words were cryptic.

"When the silver-eyed guardian walks, the past shall rise.

When the lost shadow returns, the empire shall fall.

And when the seeker finds the truth, the truth shall seek them back."

Kanvi felt the weight of the words press down on her.

"This doesn't tell us anything specific," Rama muttered, frowning.

"It tells us enough," Devi Amara said gravely. "You were never supposed to know this prophecy. And yet, now that you do, something… or someone… will come for you."

Kanvi's heartbeat quickened.

"So what do we do?" Sharada asked, arms crossed.

Devi Amara leaned back and simply said, "Solve the mystery before it solves you."

That was all the encouragement Rama needed.

"Aha! Now we are truly detectives!" he grinned. "Come, my dear assistants, we must uncover this secret before the secret uncovers us!"

Sharada rolled her eyes. "If we die because of your curiosity, I swear, Rama—"

"Yes, yes, my love," he interrupted. "Then you shall haunt me forever. Now, let's go!"

Over the next few days, they searched through ancient records, spoke to forgotten scholars, and even bribed the palace cooks with extra sweets for rumours.

Slowly, a story emerged.

Hundreds of years ago, a secret sect existed within Vijayanagar—known as The Keepers of Shadows. Their duty was to guard a hidden truth, one so dangerous that even kings feared it.

The last known Keeper had vanished mysteriously, taking the secret with him. But now… it seemed he had returned.

"The Silver-Eyed Guardian," Kanvi murmured.

"And if he has returned," Rama added, "it means whatever secret he was guarding is no longer asleep."

That night, as they pieced together the final clues, a realization hit Kanvi.

"We were never supposed to know any of this."

"And yet," Sharada said grimly, "here we are."

They had pulled back a curtain that should have remained closed. They had found answers to a question no one was supposed to ask.

And now the past was waking up.

The next morning, just as the sun rose, the Silver-Eyed Guardian appeared.

But this time, he wasn't alone.

Dozens of cloaked figures emerged from the shadows, surrounding them. The streets were empty—almost as if the city itself had sensed danger and disappeared.

Kanvi's breath hitched. Rama and Sharada stood frozen.

The Guardian finally spoke.

"You should not have looked."

"Well," Rama said nervously, "we have a habit of sticking our noses where they don't belong."

"And now you will pay the price." The Guardian raised his hand—

But just as something dark and unnatural began to swirl around them—

BOOM!

A temple bell rang loudly, cutting through the silence. The Guardian winced, as if the sound physically hurt him. The other cloaked figures shrank back, their forms quivering as if struggling to hold their shape.

Kanvi's heart pounded. What was happening?

"That sound... they hate it," she realized.

Rama, ever the genius when it came to chaos, immediately grabbed Kanvi's arm. "RUN!"

Sharada didn't need to be told twice. They bolted.

The streets of Vijayanagar had never felt longer. The Guardian's followers gave chase, their footsteps eerily silent despite their speed. They moved like shadows, unnatural and fluid.

As they neared the temple, Rama suddenly grabbed a passing fruit vendor's cart and shoved it behind them, sending mangoes rolling everywhere.

One of the shadowy figures tripped. Another slipped on a particularly juicy mango.

"Never underestimate the power of fruit!" Rama yelled triumphantly.

They dashed through the temple gates just as the priest struck the bell again. The shadowy figures froze, unable to step inside.

The Guardian glared at them from the temple steps. His silver eyes glowed. "You cannot hide forever."

And just like that, he and his followers vanished into the darkness.

For the next few days, life in Vijayanagar returned to its usual routine.

Kanvi, Rama, and Sharada pretended nothing had happened.

Rama returned to solving ridiculous court cases, like deciding whether a man could legally own a cloud. (The answer, in case anyone was wondering, was no.)

Sharada continued to scold Rama for being a walking disaster, though now with a slight edge of worry.

Kanvi tried to focus on her books, but she couldn't shake the feeling that something was still watching them.

The Guardian had disappeared. His shadowy figures had melted into the city. But deep in her gut, Kanvi knew—

"This isn't over."

One evening, as Rama was dramatically arguing with Sharada over whether his intelligence was a divine gift or a curse, Kanvi decided to take a walk.

The streets were quiet. Too quiet.

A chill ran down her spine.

And then—she saw it.

A symbol, etched into the stone wall of an alley.

The same lotus symbol she had seen in her dreams.

Her breath hitched. This was no coincidence. The prophecy, the Silver-Eyed Guardian, the shadows… something was still coming.

And this time, she feared they wouldn't be able to run.

"Every mystery has an end, but some endings are only new beginnings."

Kanvi stared at the lotus symbol carved into the alley wall, her pulse quickening. This was the same mark from her dreams, the same one tied to the prophecy.

She traced the grooves of the carving, feeling the rough stone beneath her fingers. And then—

A gust of cold air rushed past her.

The streetlights flickered. A shadow moved behind her.

Kanvi spun around, her heart hammering—but no one was there.

"This isn't over," she whispered.

The Secret Hidden in the Past

Determined to find the truth once and for all, Kanvi dragged Rama and Sharada to the royal library the next morning. The librarian, now visibly exhausted from their constant visits, sighed as they entered.

"What now, Pandit-ji?" he groaned.

"Ah, my dear guardian of books," Rama declared, "We merely seek the secrets of history to prevent our tragic demise!"

Sharada rolled her eyes. "Ignore him. We need records on the Keepers of Shadows."

The librarian frowned. "That knowledge is forbidden."

"Then why do you have books about it?" Kanvi shot back.

The librarian hesitated. Then, with a reluctant sigh, he led them to a hidden section of the library—one only a few people knew existed.

Inside, they found an ancient manuscript bound in black leather. The title read:

"The Order of the Silver Eyes."

Kanvi's breath caught as she flipped through the pages.

And there it was.

The truth they had been searching for.

The Truth behind the Prophecy

Hundreds of years ago, there existed a hidden sect known as The Keepers of Shadows. Their duty was to guard a powerful relic—one that held knowledge so dangerous it could destroy the empire.

The Silver-Eyed Guardian was the last of these Keepers. His mission? To ensure no one ever uncovered the relic.

"But what is the relic?" Kanvi murmured.

Her fingers trembled as she turned the final page—

And her heart stopped.

It wasn't gold. It wasn't jewels.

It was a book.

A book that contained the future.

The Chronicle of Fate.

"It is said that whoever reads from the Chronicle learns what is to come," the manuscript stated. "But knowledge of the future comes at a cost. It warps destiny, bending the world to its words. And in doing so… it destroys everything."

Kanvi's breath hitched.

"The prophecy never spoke of destruction because of war or betrayal," she realized. "It was about the danger of knowing the future itself."

Rama whistled. "So, in simple terms, if someone gets their hands on this book…"

"They could control fate," Sharada finished grimly.

They looked at each other.

And they knew—

Someone had already found it.

That night, under the cover of darkness, the trio returned to the old shrine where they had first encountered the Guardian.

The air was heavy. The shadows felt thicker.

And then—he appeared.

The Silver-Eyed Guardian stood before them, his cloak billowing as if caught in an unseen wind.

"You should not have come," he said.

"We know the truth," Kanvi said boldly. "The prophecy wasn't about war. It was about the Chronicle of Fate."

For the first time, the Guardian's expression shifted.

"Where is it?" Sharada demanded.

The Guardian sighed. "It does not matter. The one who has taken it… has already begun reading."

Kanvi's blood ran cold.

"Who?"

The Guardian's silver eyes darkened. "The man who seeks to rewrite destiny itself—a traitor within Vijayanagar own court."

Rama's face paled. "Oh, Maharaj is not going to like this."

The next morning, Rama, Kanvi, and Sharada rushed to the royal court.

King Krishna Devaraya sat on his throne, unaware of the danger lurking within his own walls.

"Maharaj!" Rama exclaimed. "There is a traitor among us!"

The court gasped. Ministers whispered.

"A bold claim, Rama," the king said. "Who dares betray Vijayanagar?"

Kanvi took a deep breath.

"Minister Keshava," she said.

A stunned silence filled the room.

The minister in question—a man known for his cunning mind—rose to his feet, his face calm.

"An interesting accusation," he said smoothly. "And what proof do you have?"

Rama smirked. "Ah, my dear Minister, you see, we have a small problem. The Chronicle of Fate has gone missing. And only someone with access to the royal library could have stolen it."

The king's gaze hardened. "Is this true?"

Minister Keshava laughed softly. Too softly.

"Truth," he murmured, "is merely a matter of perspective."

And then—

With a sharp flick of his wrist, he pulled out an ancient book wrapped in golden chains.

The Chronicle of Fate.

The court erupted in chaos.

"With this," Keshava said, his voice cold, "I will shape Vijayanagar destiny as I see fit. I will rewrite history, make myself ruler, and erase all who stand in my way."

King Krishna Devaraya rose from his throne, fury in his eyes.

"You dare defy the empire?"

Keshava smirked. "I am not defying it, Maharaj. I am simply… improving it."

Rama sighed. "Oh, why do villains always monologue?"

And then—Keshava opened the book.

The air shifted. The very fabric of reality wavered.

Time itself began to bend.

"We have to stop him!" Kanvi yelled.

But **how do you fight someone who holds the future in their hands?**

Then, suddenly—**an idea.**

"The bell," Kanvi whispered. *"Just like before."*

She turned to Rama. *"Ring the temple bells! Now!"*

Without hesitation, Rama grabbed a ceremonial gong from the courtroom and **smashed it against the floor.**

BOOOOOOM!

The sound **rippled through the chamber** like a shockwave.

Keshava **screamed**, clutching his ears. The book **shuddered in his hands**—and then, as if struck by a divine force—

It vanished.

Reality **snapped back into place.**

The air **settled.**

And Minister Keshava **collapsed to the ground, defeated.**

With the book gone, **time returned to normal.**

The Silver-Eyed Guardian appeared one last time, his form flickering like a fading memory.

"The Chronicle is beyond reach now," he said. *"You have saved the empire."*

And with that—**he disappeared.**

As they returned home, Sharada shook her head. "You nearly got us killed, Rama."

Rama grinned. "Ah, but my love, isn't life more exciting this way?"

Kanvi chuckled. The mystery was over.

Chapter 7

Home, but Changed

"We never truly leave the places that change us. A part of us stays behind, and a part of them stays with us."

Vijayanagar was safe. The Chronicle of Fate was gone. Minister Keshava had been imprisoned, and the Silver-Eyed Guardian had vanished.

Everything was back to normal

Everything… except Kanvi.

She had come to this world through mystery. But now, she had a new mystery of her own—

"How do I go back?"

One evening, as the sun dipped below the golden domes of Vijayanagar, Kanvi sat alone in Rama's courtyard, staring at the sky.

She had grown attached to this place.

To Rama and his ridiculous wisdom. To Sharada and her endless scolding. To the thrill of solving problems with laughter and wit.

And yet… this was not her world.

"What are you thinking, poetess?" Rama asked, stepping beside her.

Kanvi sighed. "I don't belong here, Rama."

Rama, for once, didn't joke. "I know."

Sharada joined them, arms crossed. "So, how do we send you back?"

"That," Kanvi admitted, "is the problem."

She had arrived through a dream, a vision, and a mystery. There was no portal, no doorway, and no magic spell that had brought her here.

And yet, there had to be a way.

"Sometimes, the path home is not found—it is chosen," Rama said thoughtfully.

Kanvi turned to him. "What do you mean?"

He smiled. "Perhaps your heart brought you here. And perhaps… it will take you back."

The Key to the Past… and the Future

That night, as Kanvi lay in bed, she found herself drawn to something.

A faint glow flickered across the room.

She sat up—and saw it.

The lotus symbol she had first seen, now appearing on the floor beneath her feet.

A soft whisper filled the air.

"You have solved the past. Now, it is time to return to the future."

Kanvi took a deep breath.

She turned to Rama and Sharada one last time.

"Will I ever see you again?" she asked.

Sharada smirked. "If fate is as dramatic as you are, probably."

Rama grinned. "Besides, history repeats itself. Who's to say we won't meet in another time?"

Kanvi smiled.

And as she stepped onto the glowing symbol, she whispered her final words—

"Thank you… for everything."

The world blurred.

The golden city of Vijayanagar faded.

And then—

She was gone.

When Kanvi opened her eyes, she was back.

Back in her own bed.

Back in her own time.

The modern world buzzed around her. The sounds of the city, the hum of life as she had known it.

But something was different.

She reached for a book on her desk, flipping through the pages. A history of Vijayanagar.

And there—a sketch.

A sketch of a **RAMA AND SHARADA**

Kanvi's breath caught.

"Was it real?"

A soft chuckle echoed in her mind—Rama's voice.

"Poetess, do you really need an answer?"

Kanvi smiled.

Some mysteries weren't meant to be solved.

Some were meant to be lived.

"Time is not a straight path—it is a circle, and in the end, we always return to where we began."

Kanvi sat at her desk, staring at her history book, heart still racing. She had just **returned from Vijayanagar**, from a time where she had solved an ancient prophecy, met legendary figures, and uncovered secrets that had remained buried for centuries.

"Was it real?" she whispered.

But before she could dwell on it, she heard **familiar voices** coming from the kitchen.

"Rama, stop eating before dinner!"

"Ah, my dear wife, is it a crime to admire you're cooking up close?"

Kanvi **froze.**

She knew that tone. That **exact** sarcastic reply.

She rushed out of her room and **stopped dead** in her tracks.

There, standing in her modern kitchen, was **Sharada.**

Or rather—her **mother.**

And beside her, stuffing a piece of sweet into his mouth, was **Rama.**

Or rather—her **father.**

Her **eyes widened.** Her **brain short-circuited.**

"WHAT."

Her parents turned to her **with the most casual expressions.**

"Oh, you're back?" her mother said, flipping a dosa on the stove.

Her father grinned. "Took you long enough!"

Kanvi **couldn't breathe.**

"Wait. Wait. WAIT!" she yelled, grabbing a chair before she collapsed. "You—you two—are—"

Her mother gave her a **knowing smile.** "Surprise!"

"This is a dream. This has to be a dream." Kanvi muttered, rubbing her temples. "There is NO WAY that my parents are actually Tenali Rama and Sharada Devi."

Her father—**Rama, because HOW was this even possible?!**—chuckled, stuffing another sweet into his mouth. "Well, technically, we've always been your parents. But yes, I was once that Rama."

Her mother—**Sharada, who now made even more sense!**—smirked. "And I have **always** been your mother, even when I had to deal with your father's nonsense 500 years ago."

Kanvi's jaw **dropped.**

"500 YEARS?! HOW?!"

Her father sighed dramatically. "Ah, my dear poetess, when you solve a prophecy, sometimes **the universe decides to give you another one.**"

Her mother shook her head. "It's quite simple. After the events in Vijayanagar, we were given a choice—stay there or move forward. And so…"

"Here we are!" Rama finished, grinning.

Kanvi **blinked rapidly.**

"So you're telling me… you two have just been… here? As my **normal** parents?!"

Her mother raised an eyebrow. "What did you think? That your real parents were coincidentally as chaotic as us?"

Her father smirked. "Come on, Kuku. Did you really think **you**—someone who constantly gets

dragged into historical mysteries—was born to
ordinary pcople?"

Kanvi **felt dizzy.**

Her life—**her ENTIRE life**—had been a LIE.

Kanvi groaned and dropped her head onto the table.

"So… I wasn't dreaming. Vijayanagar was real. The
prophecy was real. The Silver-Eyed Guardian was
real."

Her father popped another sweet into his mouth.
"Oh yes, all very real."

"AND YOU TWO WERE ACTUALLY
MARRIED 500 YEARS AGO?!"

IIcr mother sighed. "Unfortunately, yes."

"HEY!" Rama gasped. "You still married me
TWICE!"

Sharada smirked. "One of my **greatest regrets.**"

Kanvi groaned louder. **This was too much.**

She had time-travelled. Solved an ancient mystery.
And now her own parents were immortals who

had apparently decided to "surprise" her with this information?!

"This is NOT how I expected my life to go," she mumbled.

Her father grinned. "Ah, but **when has your life ever been normal?**"

Kanvi opened her mouth—then paused.

He had a point.

Kanvi stood there, arms crossed, pretending to be furious. Her eyes were slightly red, her lips pressed into a thin line, but her stance was firm.

"So, you two just casually decided to drop the biggest truth of my life over dinner? Like, 'Oh, pass the salt, by the way, we're immortal'?! WHAT KIND OF PARENTS DO THAT?"

Rama, ever the troublemaker, sighed dramatically. "Ah, my dear poetess, if I had known this would upset you so much, I would've made laddoos first."

Sharada smacked him on the arm. "FOCUS, Rama!"

Kanvi clenched her fists. "Do you know how insane this is?! How could you keep this from me?! I almost DIED!"

Her voice cracked slightly at the last word, and before she could stop herself, a **single tear slipped down her cheek.** She angrily wiped it away, but it was too late.

Her parents saw it.

And before Kanvi could react, she was **wrapped in the tightest, warmest, most ridiculous hug of her life.**

Rama and Sharada **squeezed her from both sides**, nearly suffocating her between them.

"Ah, my precious daughter!" Rama wailed. "Do not cry! You will ruin your poetic reputation!"

"You idiot," Sharada muttered, her voice softer now, her chin resting on Kanvi's head. "We never wanted to keep you in the dark. We were just… waiting for the right time."

Kanvi let out a muffled groan. "I CAN'T BREATHE."

"Let her go, Rama," Sharada scolded.

"YOU'RE ALSO HOLDING ME TOO TIGHT!" Kanvi gasped.

Sharada cleared her throat and barely loosened her grip. "Well, I have some emotions too, you know."

Kanvi blinked, startled. **Sharada Devi—her usually fierce, no-nonsense mother—was tearing up.**

And that broke her.

With a dramatic sigh, she finally gave in, wrapping her arms around both of them.

"Fine," she mumbled into their shoulders. "I guess I love you both. A little."

Rama gasped. "A LITTLE?!"

Kanvi smirked. "Fine, maybe a lot. But you're still the most chaotic parents in existence."

Sharada wiped her eyes and pulled back, **pinching Kanvi's cheek.** "And you're our biggest headache."

Rama ruffled her hair. "Ah, but the best headache in history!"

Kanvi groaned but laughed, her heart feeling **lighter than ever.**

Because no matter how insane her life was…

She had them.

And that was **enough.**

"Some stories never end… they simply change the chapter."

"We never truly leave the places that change us,"

"In every lifetime, we find the ones we love. Over and over again.

As Kanvi lay in bed that night, she whispered to herself:

"Some people search their whole lives for adventure. But for me? Adventure found me."

And with that thought, she **closed her eyes… and smiled.**

Because **this** was just the beginning.

The beginning of a life where anything was possible.

Note

"Writing this story with **Dr. S.T. NAIDU** has been an incredible journey. Together, we shared ideas, created unforgettable characters, and built a world that we hope touched your hearts. Every late-night brainstorming session, every edit, and every discussion brought this book to life. Thank you for being part of this adventure!"

The next chapter awaits… See you in **Book 2!**

With gratitude and excitement

LAASHYA NAIDU & Dr.S.T.NAIDU

"Some endings are only the start of a new legend."

Coming soon: **Rivani**

www.ingramcontent.com/pod-product-compliance
Lightning Source LLC
Chambersburg PA
CBHW062228150726
47991CB00006B/2491